ISBN 1 85854 527 7
© Brimax Books Ltd 1997. All rights reserved.
Published by Brimax Books Ltd, Newmarket,
England, CB8 7AU, 1997.
Printed in Spain.

A Little Bit SCARY!

Written by Gill Davies   Illustrated by Gill Guile

BRIMAX

INTRODUCTION

"There's no such thing as monsters,
You just dream of them at night."
That's what people tell me;
But are they really right?

"Witches don't exist at all!"
That's what my mother said.
So who is it that snores and cackles
Underneath my bed?

And who's the creature in the closet
All fat and pink and floppy?
He has six arms which wave at me
And a smile that's wet and soppy.

And then there is the Yellow Thing
Who peeps around my door.
I can only see one hairy arm
And a curve of orange claw.

The Purple Beastie with green eyes
Hangs by the window pane,
His face is long and stretched and sad;
Eyes weeping with the rain.

The tiny, fluffy ghost is shy;
She hides behind the clock.
She jumps up every time it chimes
Hiccuping with shock.

Who says there are no monsters?
I have met them many times,
Along with countless ghosts and ghouls
Who live inside my rhymes!

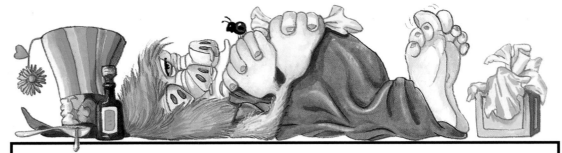

THE MONSTER WITH FIVE NOSES

Next time you have a cough or cold
It's not as bad as one supposes;
Just think how terrible it must be
For the monster with five noses.

He has a lot of handkerchiefs
To wave about his face.
But he never knows in time which nose
Will ATISHOO! around the place.

The monster with five noses
Has hands that number four.
So although he wipes his noses,
There is always just one more.

So next time you have a cough or cold
We hope you'll sympathise
With that sorry, sneezing creature
Whose noses number five.

WEREWOLF

When werewolf goes out on the town
He wears a dinner suit.
And he likes it if you scratch his ears
And tell him he is cute.

The werewolf never knows
If he will be dog or man.
So deciding what to feed him
Can be difficult to plan.

Sometimes he fancies bones
And sometimes eggs and peas.
And if you peek when saying grace
You may catch him scratching fleas.

Sometimes he eats with a knife and fork
But he might dip in a claw.
And you don't know if he'll shake your hand
Or raise a hairy paw.

THE WITCH WHO LOST HER BROOMSTICK

The witch who lost her broomstick
Was worried she'd be late.
It was Halloween, and the evening
When the witches congregate.

The witch who lost her broomstick
Did not want to miss the fun;
She could hear the others laughing
And knew the party had begun.

So she flew off on a vacuum
With a dustbag at her rear.
The others said, "She's crazy!"
But she pretended not to hear.

The witch upon the vacuum said,
"There are those who'll laugh and titter;
But I fly much faster than before
And I've sucked up all the litter."

THE GIGANTIC MONSTER

When the Gigantic Monster came to stay
We offered him a bath.
"That's far too small for me," he said,
And gave a cheery laugh.
"In the country where I come from,
I have a lake that's very deep.
I need a lot more water
Than your bath could ever keep."

So we took him to the swimming pool
And he filled it on his own.
When he nosedived through the water,
It reminded him of home.
While we rubbed him dry with towels
He sang a song that made him cry
Of purple hills and caves
And water deeper than the sky.

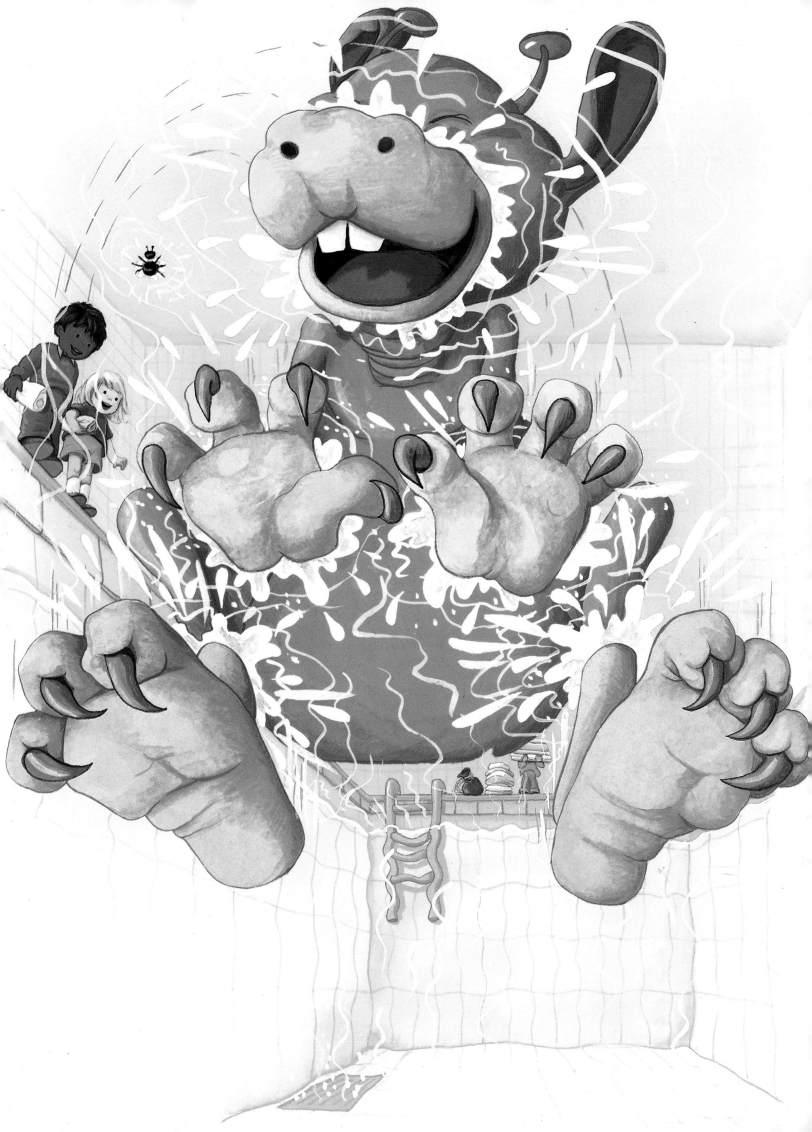

THE APOLOGETIC GHOST

The ghost who took his head off
Was really most polite;
He said, "I do not mean
To give anyone a fright.
I only walk through walls
Because it is easier to do
Than opening those silly doors
And trying to squeeze through.
I only disappear because,
In fact, I'm rather shy.
When people start to stare at me
I blush and fade and fly.
I do not mean to groan and wail
And scare my friends away;
It's just that when I talk
My voice gurgles out that way."
The ghost who took his head off said
"It isn't so alarming,
I do smile beneath my armpit,
And I'm trying to be charming."

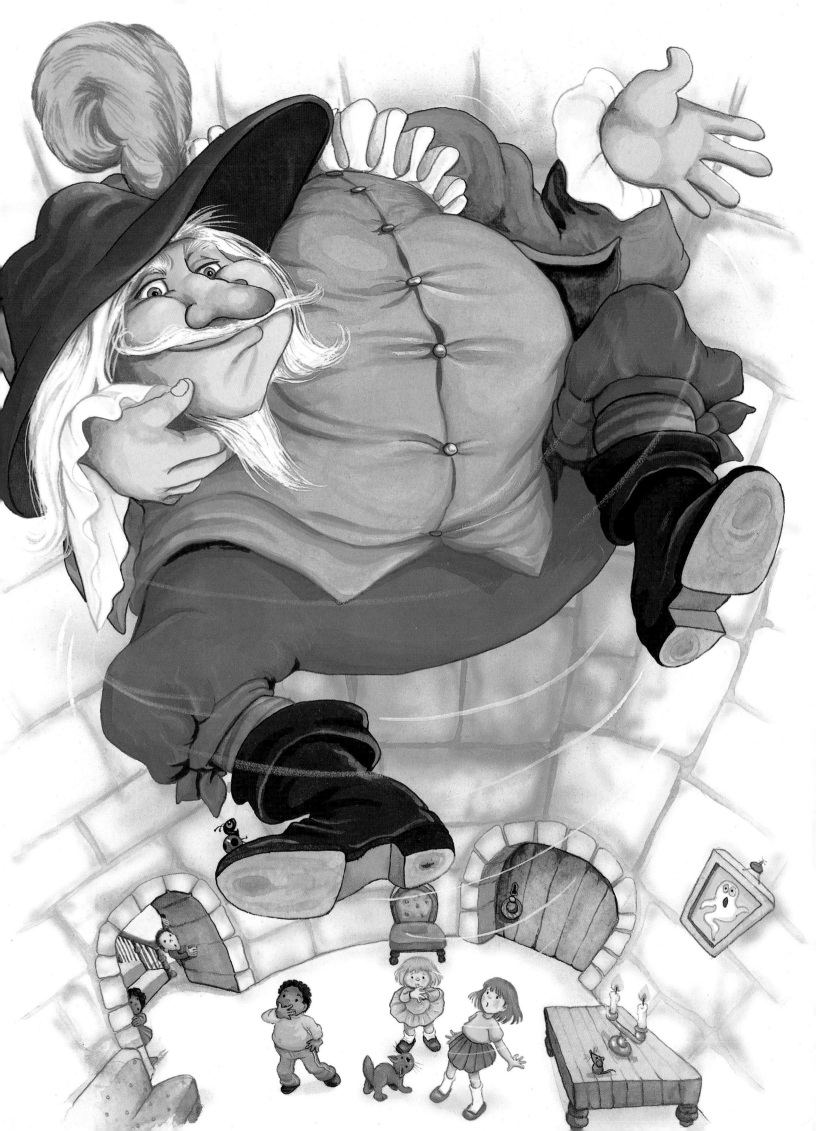

Emma's Wriggly Monster

When Emma found the wriggly monster
She hid it in her bed.
"What are those bumps beneath the quilt?"
Her curious father said.
"Oh, Daddy, they're just my knees!"
Said Emma with a smile,
And hoped the wriggly monster
Would stay still for a while.

When Father left, the monster laughed,
Then wriggled out and said,
"You'd better check if I have left
Any squiggles in the bed.
I have so many twists and turns
And loops at different angles."
"I'll unknot you," Emma said,
Unravelling the tangles.

The Vampire with False Teeth

The vampire with false teeth
Found it hard to bite.
His false fangs always wobbled
So he couldn't hang on tight.

And when he went out flying,
His bat wings stretched to soar,
The fangs kept falling out
And dropping on the floor.

The vampire with false teeth
Retired into his coffin space.
"If I lie down," he said. "My fangs
Stay in their proper place!"

MR SQUIDGE

Whenever I am bored
I go down below the bridge
And talk to my best friend,
Whose name is Mr Squidge.
Mr Squidge has long green hair
Right down to his dangly toes,
And peeping out from underneath -
A bulbous, warty nose.

But today he said, "I can't decide
If trolls should cut their hair.
Mine gets in an awful mess
With tangles everywhere."
So I took him for a haircut,
And a blow dry, and a style.
It shows off his squashy, wrinkled face
And his odd, lopsided smile.

SKELETONS

In the middle of the night
When the moon is sailing high,
The skeletons wake up,
"Let's have a ball!" they cry.

Bony plays the double bass;
A guitar Rattle strums.
Ribs dances with his castanets
While Sternum plays the drums.

The skeletons like rock and roll
And a good old-fashioned twist.
They congo around the gravestones
And tango in the mist.

Then when the dawn comes streaking
They pause to catch their breath
And say, "What a fantastic time;
The best night of our death!"

Little Yukky, Squidgy Things

I'm not afraid of giant things
Or great big dinosaurs;
Tyrannosaurus Rex is sweet
And so are sharks like Jaws.

It's little squidgy, running things
That make me ill at ease,
Like spiders, ants and beetles
And leggy centipedes.

I should happily invite
An ugly ogress in the house,
But never, never, never,
A yukky cockroach or a mouse!

FRANKENSTEIN'S MONSTER

The monster made by Frankenstein
Likes new clothes to wear.
But when he goes out shopping,
He says, "It isn't fair!

My trousers are too short,
My jacket's badly split.
I'd like designer running shoes
But nothing seems to fit.

I undress in the changing room;
Folk stare and wonder whether
I'll catch my shirt upon the bolt
That holds my neck together.

I'd like to be a modern man
In a T-shirt and blue jeans.
I'll have cosmetic surgery
To tidy up my seams."

GLUGS

There's a family of monster Glugs
Who live inside my home.
You can hear them splash and gurgle
As around the pipes they roam.

And when you pull the plug out,
They glug up in a rush,
Wanting to be first to ride
The soapy, swirly gush!

Sometimes you hear one moaning,
But they mostly laugh and sing.
They make a high-pitched whistle
When they have a gluggy fling.

If you turn the taps off quickly
It gives them quite a shock.
You hear them fall about and bang
As on the pipes they knock.

I've never actually seen a Glug,
However hard I stare
Up taps and down the plug hole,
But I can hear them giggling there.

GHOST TRAIN

The ghost train is coming,
The ghost train is coming,
In the distance it whistles twice.
Then you hear a rumble humming,
Roaring, rushing, tumble drumming,
And the night is as cold as ice.

There's a sudden gush of steam,
And the windows, spotted, gleam
Like a caterpillar on the rails.
With its ghosts and ghouls, it races,
Phantom drivers without faces,
As it hisses and roars and wails.

Then suddenly it's gone;
There is a darkness where it shone,
On its steamy, eerie midnight ride.
Train spotting can be fun,
But do not ever spot this one -
It is better to run and hide.

Mixing Spells

The witch is stirring her cauldron.
It is full of all sorts of things;
Spiders and lizards and worms
And a bug with water wings.
"The water is boiling hot today!"
Says Newt who slips over the side,
As beetles and bats and big, whiskered rats
Scuttle away and hide.

When she needs some extra magic
The witch makes special spells.
She pours in bottles of magic
Till the cauldron bubbles and swells.

She finds cobwebs from the dungeon,
A toad with a crinkled smile;
Snakes that slither and spit,
Snapping crocodiles from the Nile.
Waving her wand, she stirs the cauldron,
And dances and shrieks and cackles,
As lizards and worms tumble and squirm
And swim as the fire crackles.

Mr Hunchback

Mr Hunchback lives in Notre Dame
And haunts the great, high tower
With his friends, the stony gargoyles,
Who grimace, scowl and glower.

Sometimes in the Paris night
You hear the great bells chime.
You know that Mr Hunchback
Is having a swinging time.

He hangs about the belfry,
And sways at dizzy heights
Saying, "Ding-dong, swinging, ringing
Livens up my nights!"

Messy Monster

"Your bedroom is chaotic!"
My angry mother said.
"Dirty plates and toys and jeans
Are heaped upon the bed."

Then I knew the Messy Monster
Must have paid a visit.
Whenever he has been around,
My room looks like a bomb has hit it!

He slides clothes from off their hangers
And jumbles every drawer.
He tangles socks and scatters shoes
And books across the floor.

He never puts my toys away,
But mother says, "What rot!
You are the only monster
That this messy room has got!"

But I could never make that mess -
So much, so fast, so well.
The Messy Monster's been again
To visit, I can tell.

GIANT RIDING

I should like to meet a giant;
Not the nasty ogre kind,
But a kind and gentle giant,
You know the sort I have in mind.

He would lift me on his shoulder
And skip right over hills.
I'm sure that giant riding
Must be one of life's great thrills.

Up high, I'd hang on tightly,
While his boots, with just one stride
Would step across the ocean
To countries on the other side.

At last he'd bring me home again
And set me gently down,
Then wink and smile, and in one leap
Jump right across the town.

BLIND DATE

Mr Cyclops only had one eye,
And so he wondered whether
Medusa might not fancy him
When they had a date together.

Now Medusa, she was worried too,
For although she looked quite stunning,
Her head was full of hissing snakes
Which sent most suitors running!

Mr Cyclops said, "Medusa dear,
I find it hard to focus,
But I think those rollers in your hair
Are trying to provoke us."

"Oh you're divine," Medusa drooled.
"Blind dates I have been missing;
You and I, my one-eyed Cy,
Should spend the whole night kissing!"

WHERE HAVE ALL THE MONSTERS GONE?

They don't make gruesome monsters
Like they used to anymore:
There are no ogres shopping
In the supermarket store.
You never see a hairy beastie
Jogging down the road;
And it must be ages since a witch
Turned you - or me - into a toad.
There are no ghosts or goblins,
Not even in the dark;
And I've yet to meet a bandaged mummy
Strolling through the park.
Are all the vampires pensioned off?
Are the big, bad wolves annoyed?
Do the Things and Its from Outer Space
Mind being unemployed?
Now you don't meet gruesome monsters,
They are very rare today,
But beware! For rumour has it
A revival's on the way!